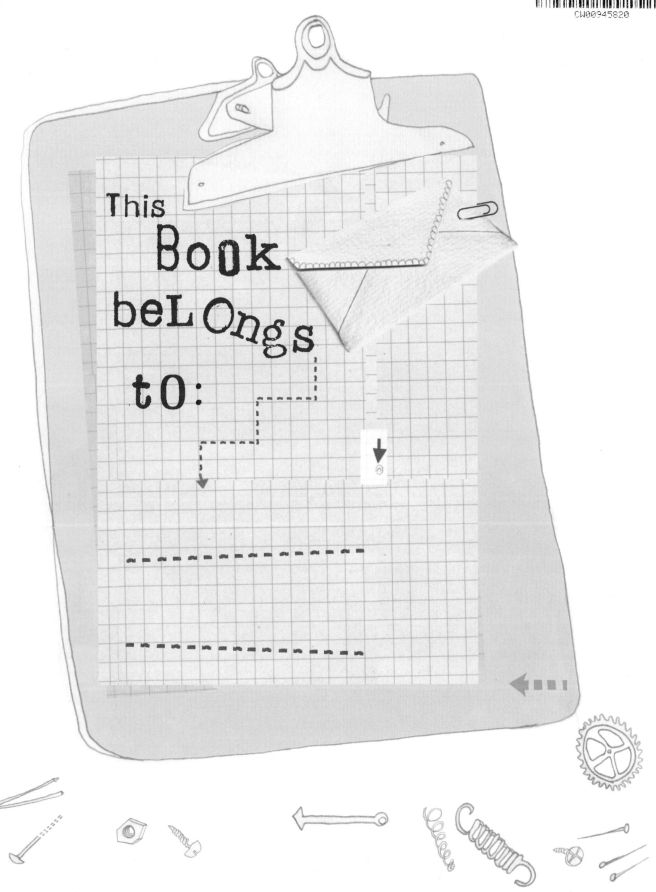

This **Book beLOngs to:**

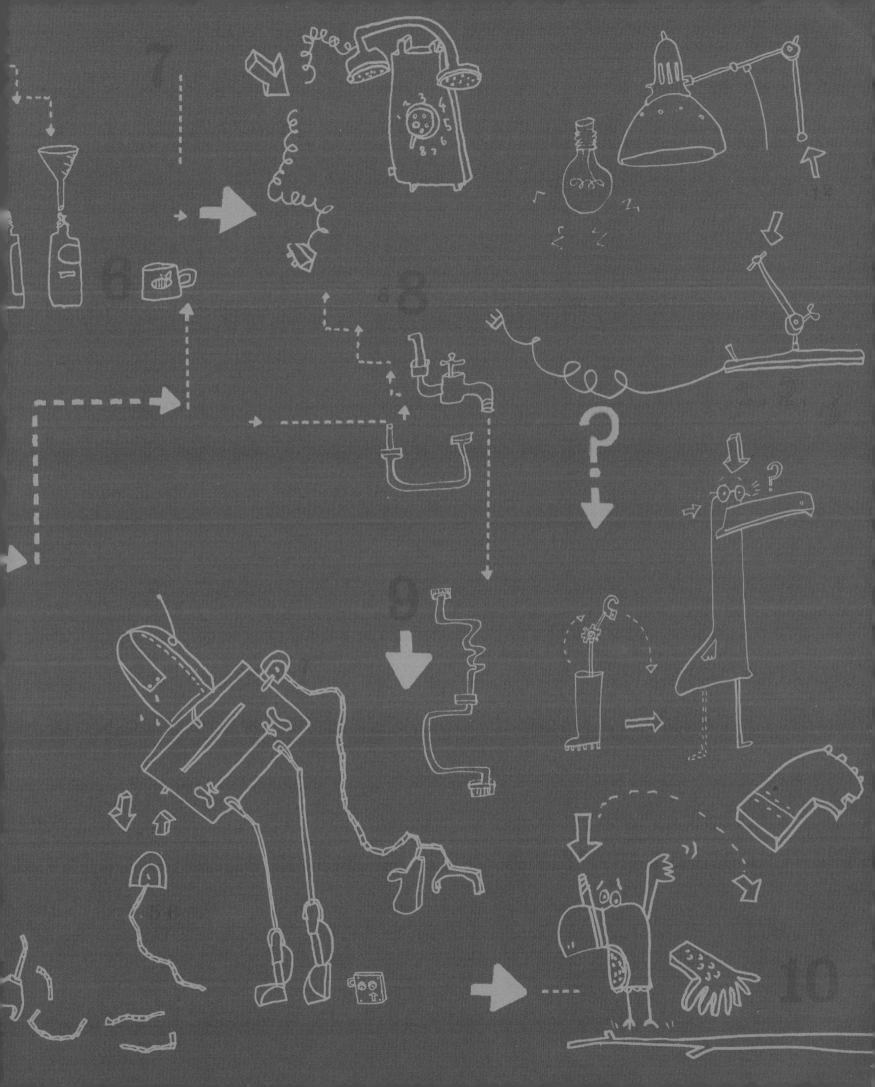

Dedicated To...

TaLking ThErapies

www.nhs.uk
Thank you

Don't worry! Now we have spoken,
I can fix what is broken!

G.c The right tool for the right job X

A TEMPLAR BOOK

First published in the UK in 2023 by Templar Books,
an imprint of Bonnier Books UK
4th Floor, Victoria House,
Bloomsbury Square, London WC1B 4DA
Owned by Bonnier Books
Sveavägen 56, Stockholm, Sweden
www.bonnierbooks.co.uk

10 9 8 7 6 5 4 3 2 1

ISBN 978-1-78741-835-6

Edited by Katie Haworth and Sophie Hallam
Designed by Genevieve Webster
Production by Nick Read
Printed in China

These characteRs are inspirEd by My family, frieNds & hisToricAL heroes.

MorE heRe → Juliapatton.co.uk

← Home

Bea's WoR shop →

The Fixer of Broken Things

1

Julia Patton

templar books

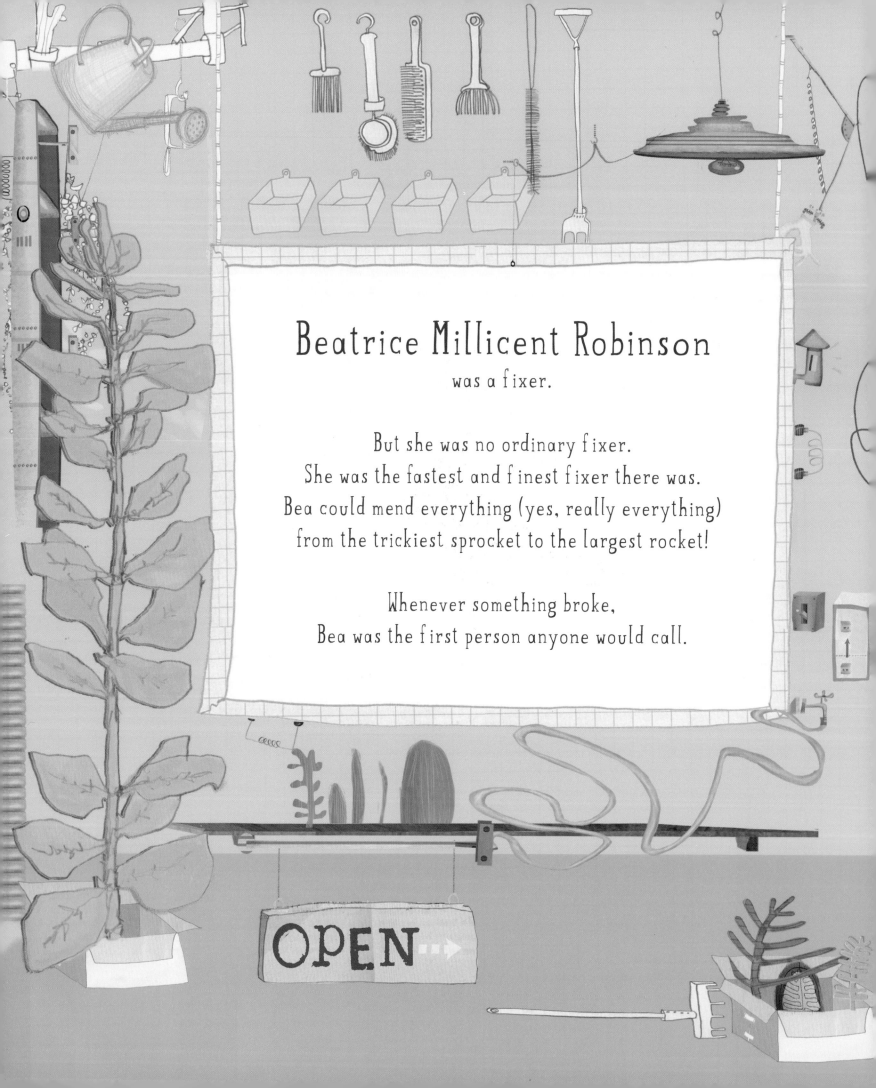

Beatrice Millicent Robinson
was a fixer.

But she was no ordinary fixer.
She was the fastest and finest fixer there was.
Bea could mend everything (yes, really everything)
from the trickiest sprocket to the largest rocket!

Whenever something broke,
Bea was the first person anyone would call.

OPEN

FiXiNG LiST

Monsieur LockhEart
↓
cLock

DR AnkiTa
↓
counting MachiNe

MR McNick
↓
MEchanicaL
ELephant

Bea fixed small tricksy things like Monsieur Lockheart's tiniest clock,
which once had a tick but now had no tock.

She swapped the springs and tightened the sprongs.
Soon the clock was as good as new.

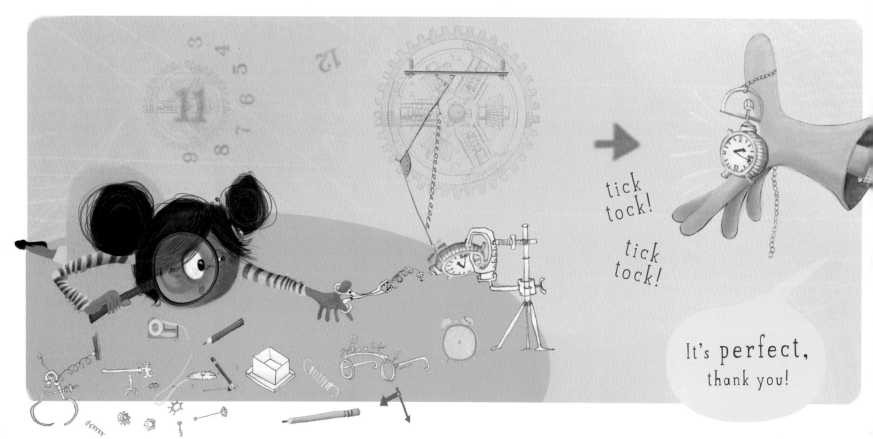

Bea could fix fiddly things like Dr Ankita's clever counting machine.

She replaced all the Os and restored all the 1s.
Dr Ankita turned some knobs and whirred the cogs.

Bea could even fix

HUMONGOUS

things like Mr McNick's marvellous mechanical elephant Sophia, whose giant legs had sadly stopped

STOMPING.

Bea! Sophia has seized up! She's **stonkered!**

STOM

STOMP!

Strapped securely in her harness, Bea's tiny hands tinkered
and tightened until Sophia's magnificent legs were stomping once again.

STOMP!

STOMP!

Bea's fame spread far and wide. She was brought

handbags

Beep beep

and helicopters,

TOAST

ⓐ

ⓑ

trains and toasters,

ⓒ

saxophones and satellites,

ⓓ

and once an entire collection of tiny robots. →

Don't worry! Now we have spoken, I can fix what is broken.

baNg baNg

TACOS

Thank you, Bea!

She fixed them all.

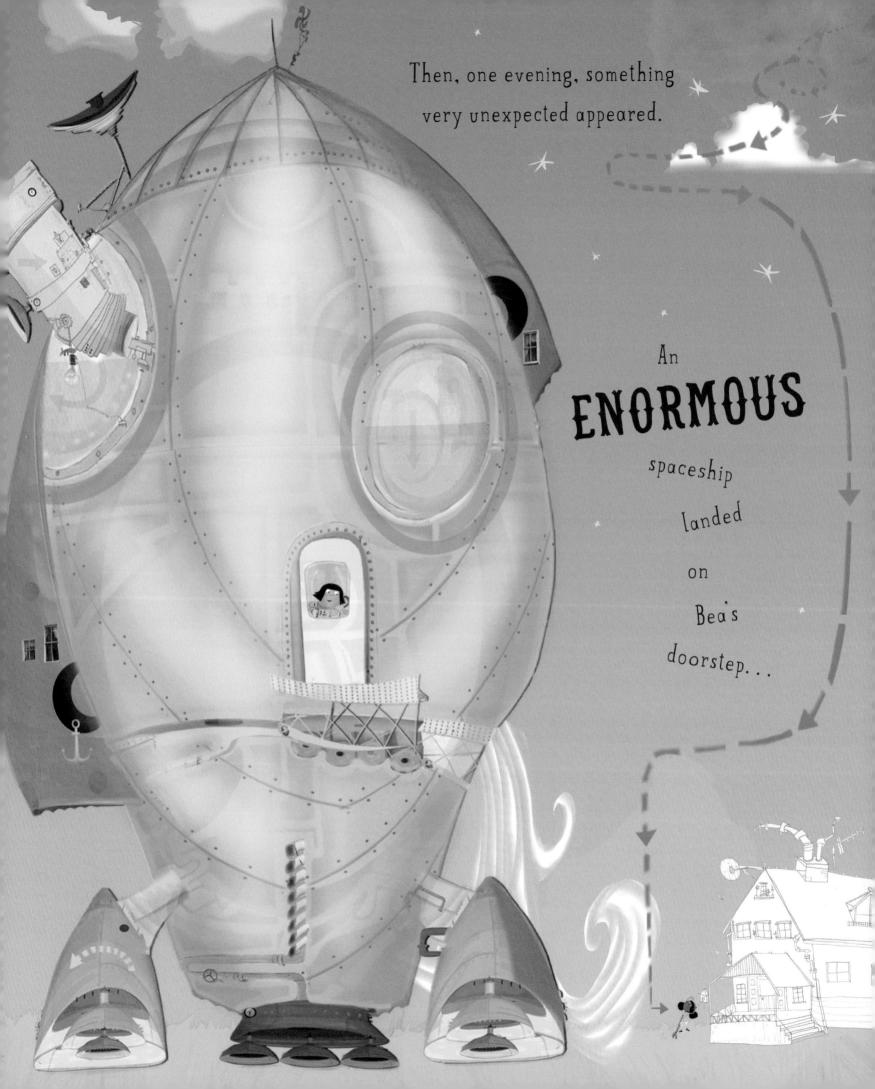

Then, one evening, something very unexpected appeared.

An **ENORMOUS** spaceship landed on Bea's doorstep...

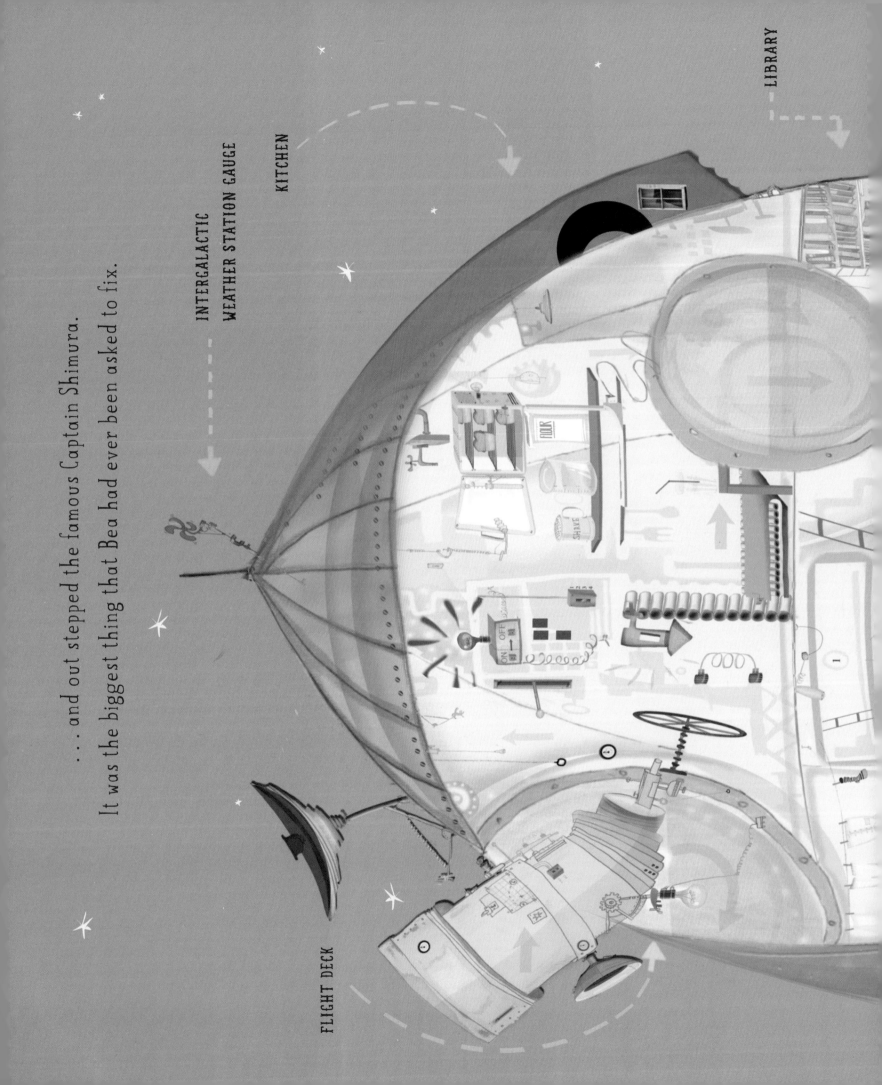

. . . and out stepped the famous Captain Shimura.

It was the biggest thing that Bea had ever been asked to fix.

INTERGALACTIC
WEATHER STATION GAUGE

KITCHEN

LIBRARY

FLIGHT DECK

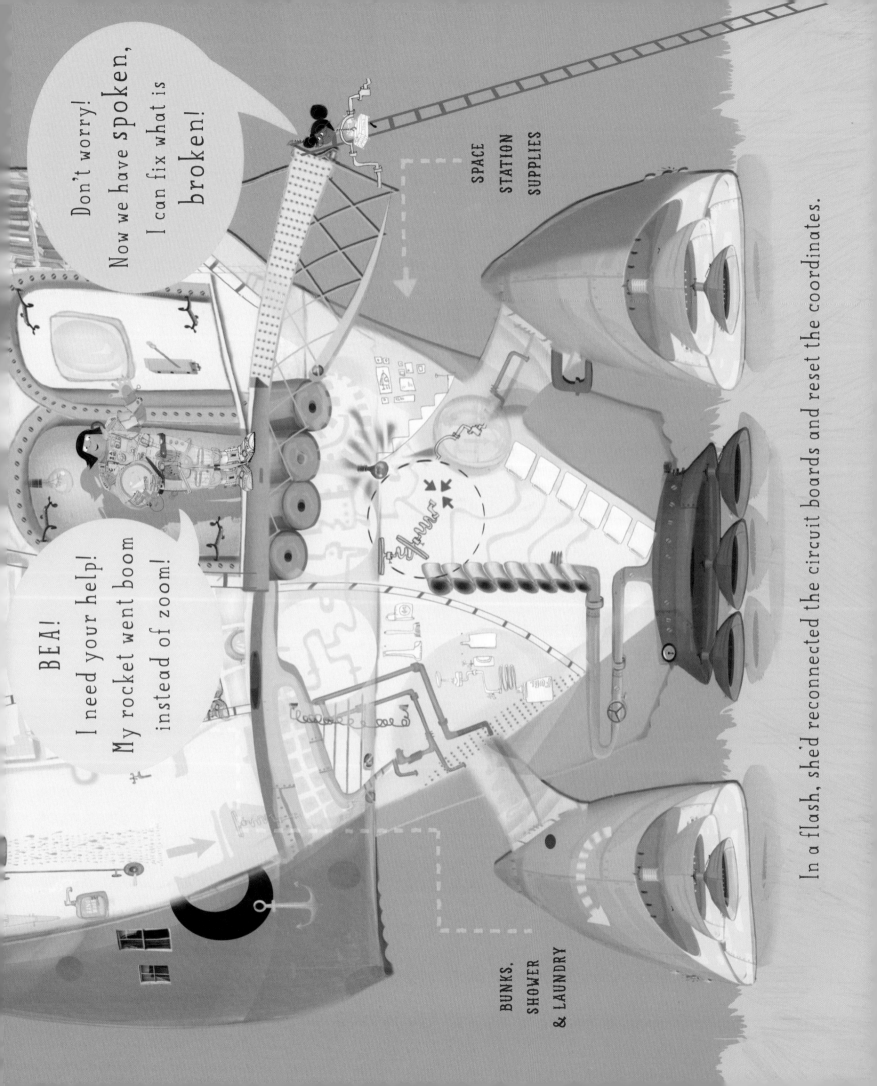

In a flash, she'd reconnected the circuit boards and reset the coordinates.

As Bea was packing away her tools she came across something she'd not seen before. She was baffled.

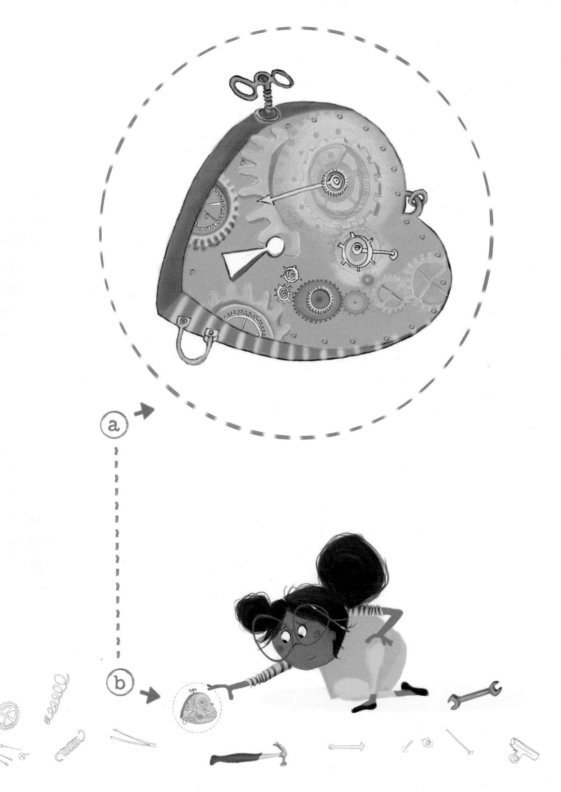

She didn't know where it had come from or what it was exactly,
but she knew from the very moment she held it close that it was broken on the inside.

Bea took the thing home and sat with it for a while...

Bea spent a whole week trying to figure out the problem.

She read big books.

She examined small parts. ⓑ

She listened very carefully.

And she rattled and wiggled the thing.

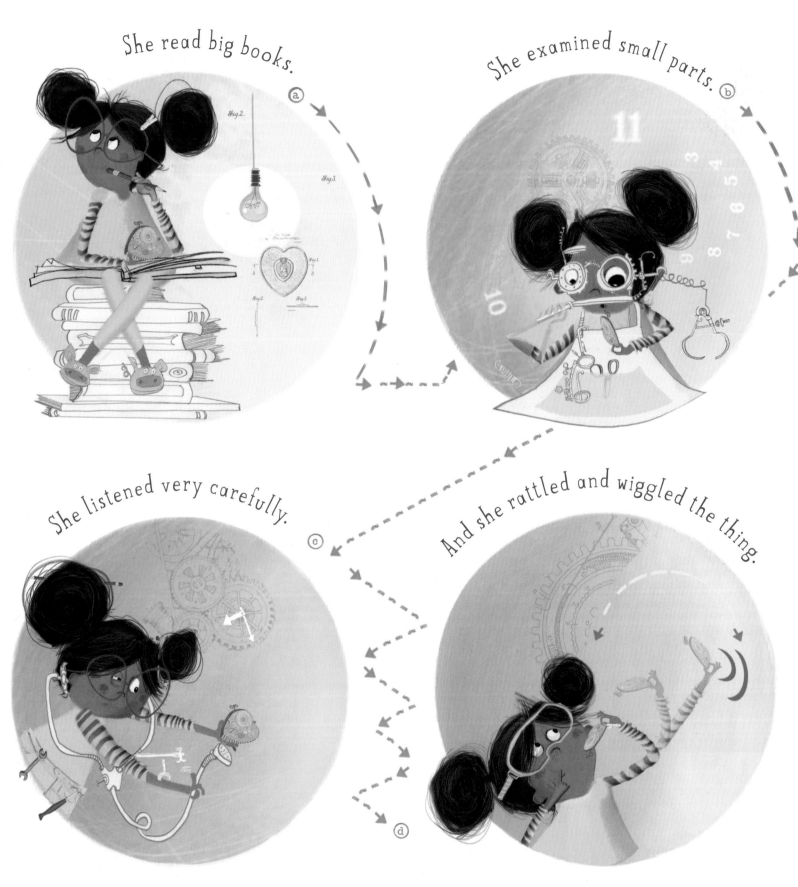

No matter what she did... it stayed quiet and still.

Bea was quiet too so Mum asked her, "Why is my little Bea not buzzing?"
But Bea didn't tell her about the broken thing.
What good was a fixer who can't fix a little problem like this?
So she said:

But she wasn't okay because the thing was still broken.
Bea slipped it into her backpack and went to see if anyone else had an answer.

Monsieur Lockheart was in his workshop.

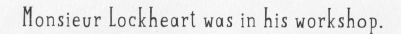

Morning Bea!
It's all **tick-tock** today!
Since you fixed my clock
it's been non-stop!

He looked much too busy to be
bothered by Bea's broken thing.

Dr Ankita was
in her laboratory.

Morning Bea!
Look at these numbers.
Thanks to you I've got a
billion possible answers
to the problem...
Now, where was I?

Bea didn't want to disturb her,
so didn't show her the broken thing.

Mr McNick was in the circus ring with Sophia who was stomping and stamping so loudly he didn't hear Bea at all.

It looked like he had much bigger things to worry about than her broken thing.

Captain Shimura was still on Mars so Bea spoke to her on the computer.

Bea it's **wonderful** here, the sands are as red as the sunset. You would love it!

It sounded so amazing that Bea didn't think the captain would be very interested in her broken thing.

Back at the workshop, Bea switched off the lights and hung up her toolbelt.

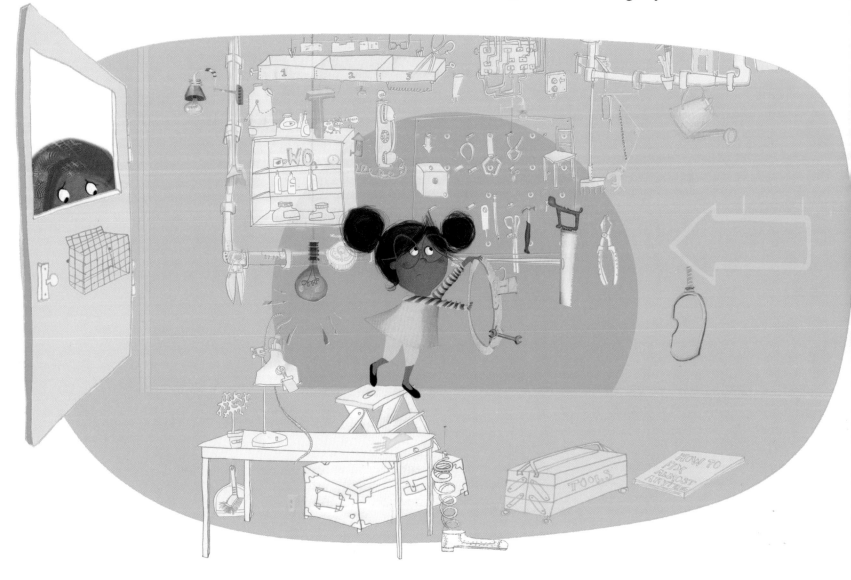

For the first time ever the happy buzz of fixing stopped.
Completely.

Bea held the broken thing in her hands.

I'm sorry. I don't know how to fix you.

But what Bea hadn't realised is that all her friends
had noticed her silence.

Mum told Monsieur Lockheart that Bea had stopped fixing.

1

2

Monsieur Lockheart told Dr Ankita.

Dr Ankita broadcast the message to Mr McNick...

3

...who used his loudest voice to call Captain Shimura...

4

...who turned around her rocket.

5

6

They all gathered outside Bea's workshop
to see how they could help.

CLOSED

WORKSHOP

There was a loud
KNOCK KNOCK
on Bea's door.

Bea went to open it,
and outside was her mum
and all her friends.
"What is it that can't be fixed
my little one?" asked Mum.

WORKSHOP

CLOSED

Bea slowly started to talk, and with many *umms* and *ahhs*, she finally held out the broken thing. Then she whispered...

I need some help please. This **heart** is **broken** and I can't **fix** it by myself.

"Thank you for sharing this with me, Bea," said Mum. "Together we can fix anything. Do you remember your own rule of fixing?"

"Now we have spoken, we can fix what is broken!"

. . . sang everyone together.

So they all looked at the thing together and began to talk...

And then something very special happened.

1

The broken thing started to gently hum.

2

Then it buzzed.

3 ⇒ Then it started to whirr...

And finally it began to beat happily in Bea's hands!

4

BA BOOM! BA BOOM! BA BOOM! BA BOOM!

Beatrice Millicent Robinson was a fixer.
But she was no ordinary fixer. Bea could mend anything...

...especially now she knew that not even a fixer
of broken things had to mend everything by herself.

In Bea's workshop, the once broken thing whirred and hummed...

... and if it ever missed a beat or seemed a little sad and quiet,

Bea knew exactly who to talk to.

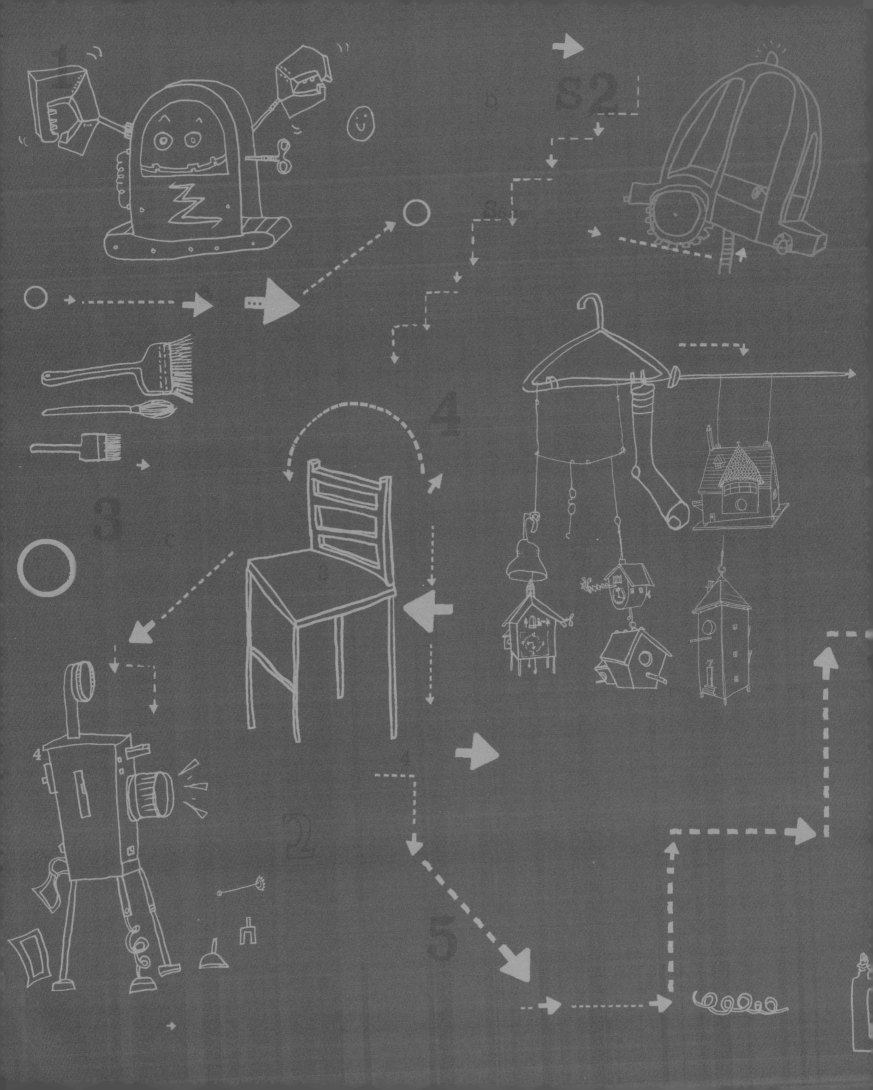

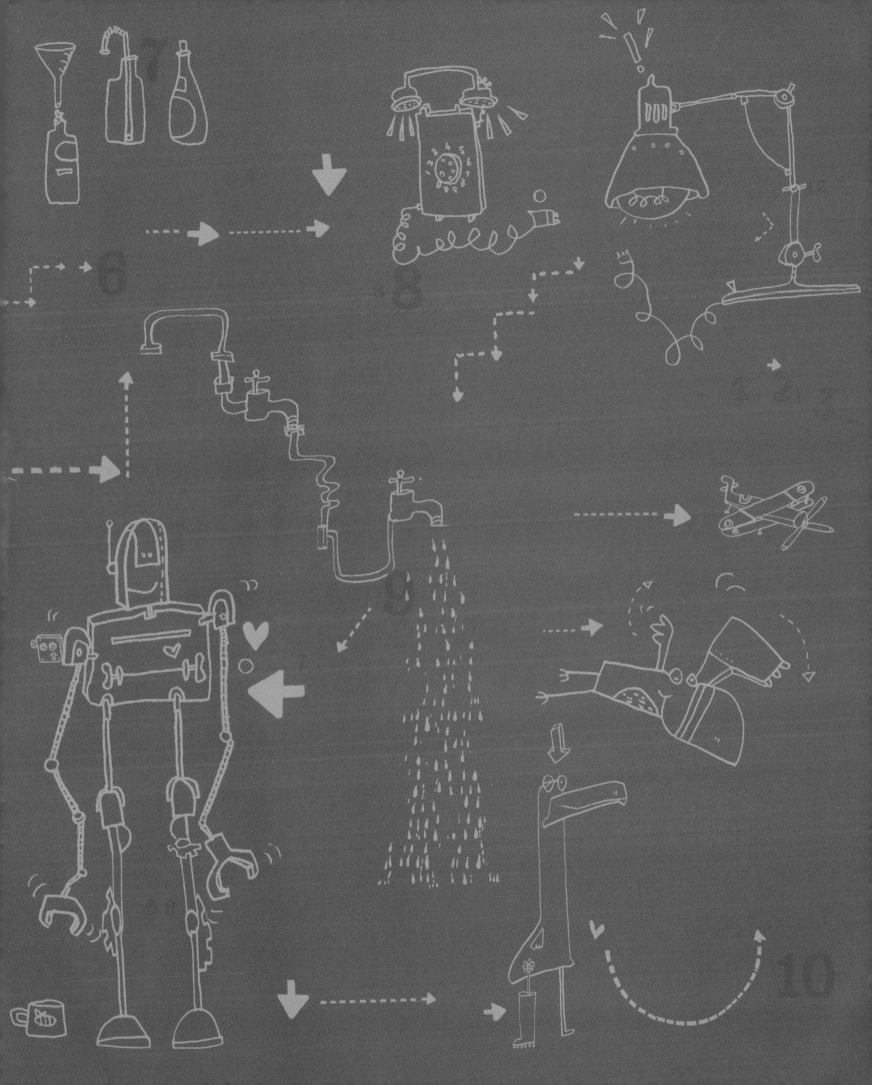

Another fantastic story of friendship
from Julia Patton

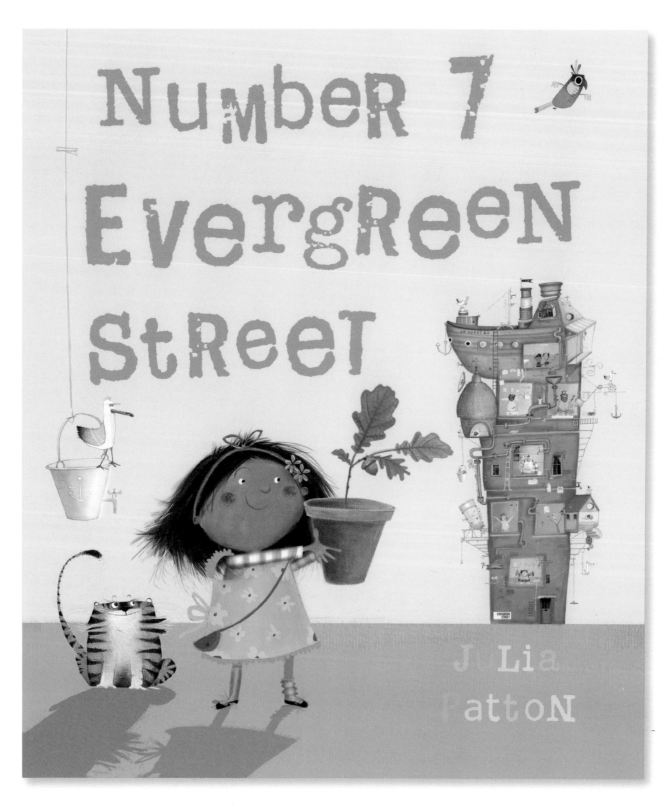

NumbeR 7 EvergReeN StReeT

JuLia PattoN